MW01079499
PARIS
FRANCE
BORDEAUX
LYON
TOULOUSE
MARSEILLE

SPAIN
LA CORUÑA
BARCELONA
MADRID
VALENCIA
SEVILLA

ALASKA
USA
SAN FRANCISCO
CHICAGO
NEW YORK
LOS ANGELES
HOUSTON
MIAMI

BEIJING
XI'AN
CHENGDU
SHANGHAI
GUANGZHOU
CHINA
中华人民共和国

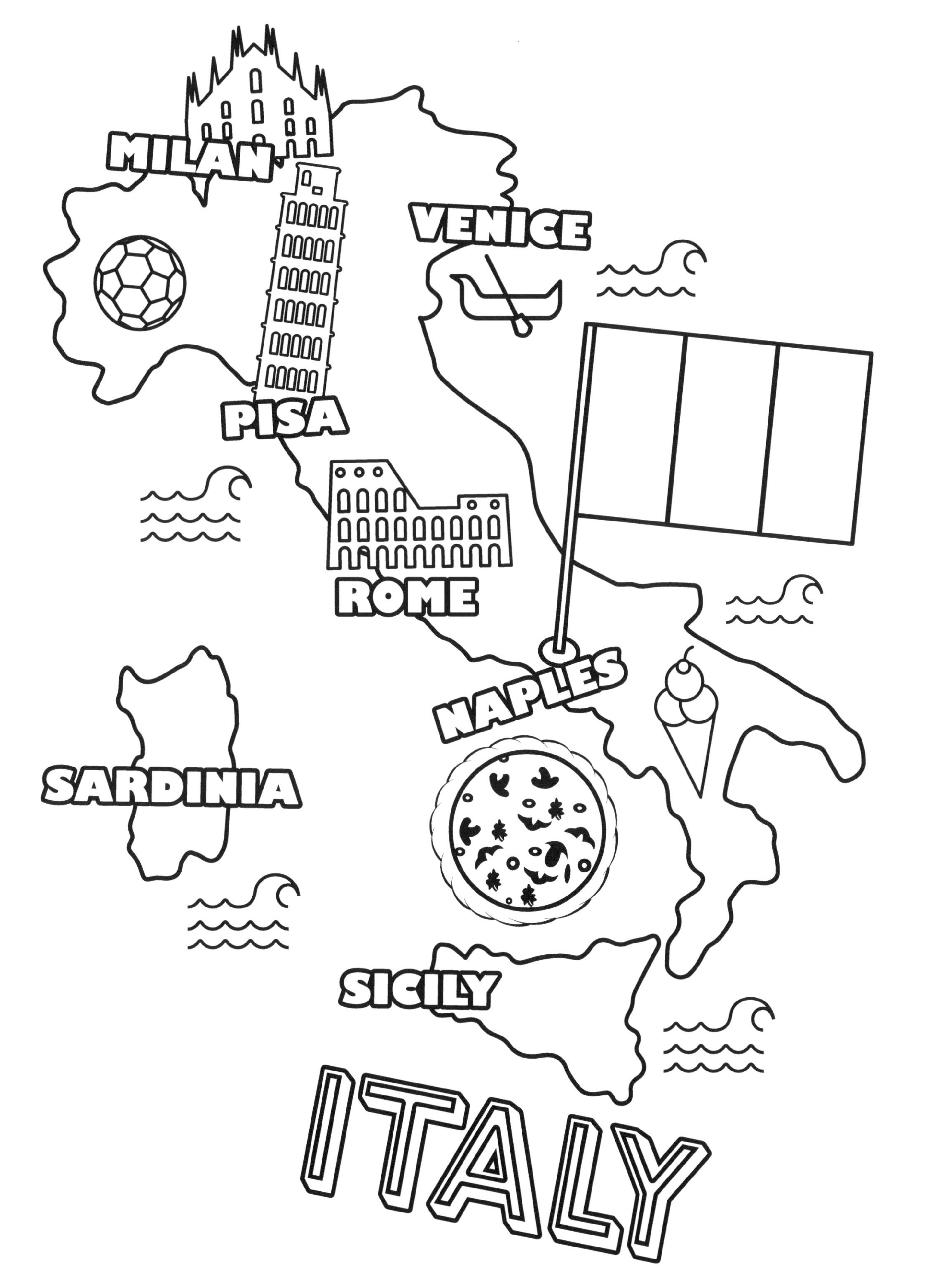
MILAN
VENICE
PISA
ROME
NAPLES
SARDINIA
SICILY
ITALY

TIJUANA
MONTERREY
GUADALAJARA
MEXICO CITY
MEXICO

HAMBURG
BERLIN
COLOGNE
GERMANY
NUREMBERG
FRANKFURT
STUTTGART
MUNICH

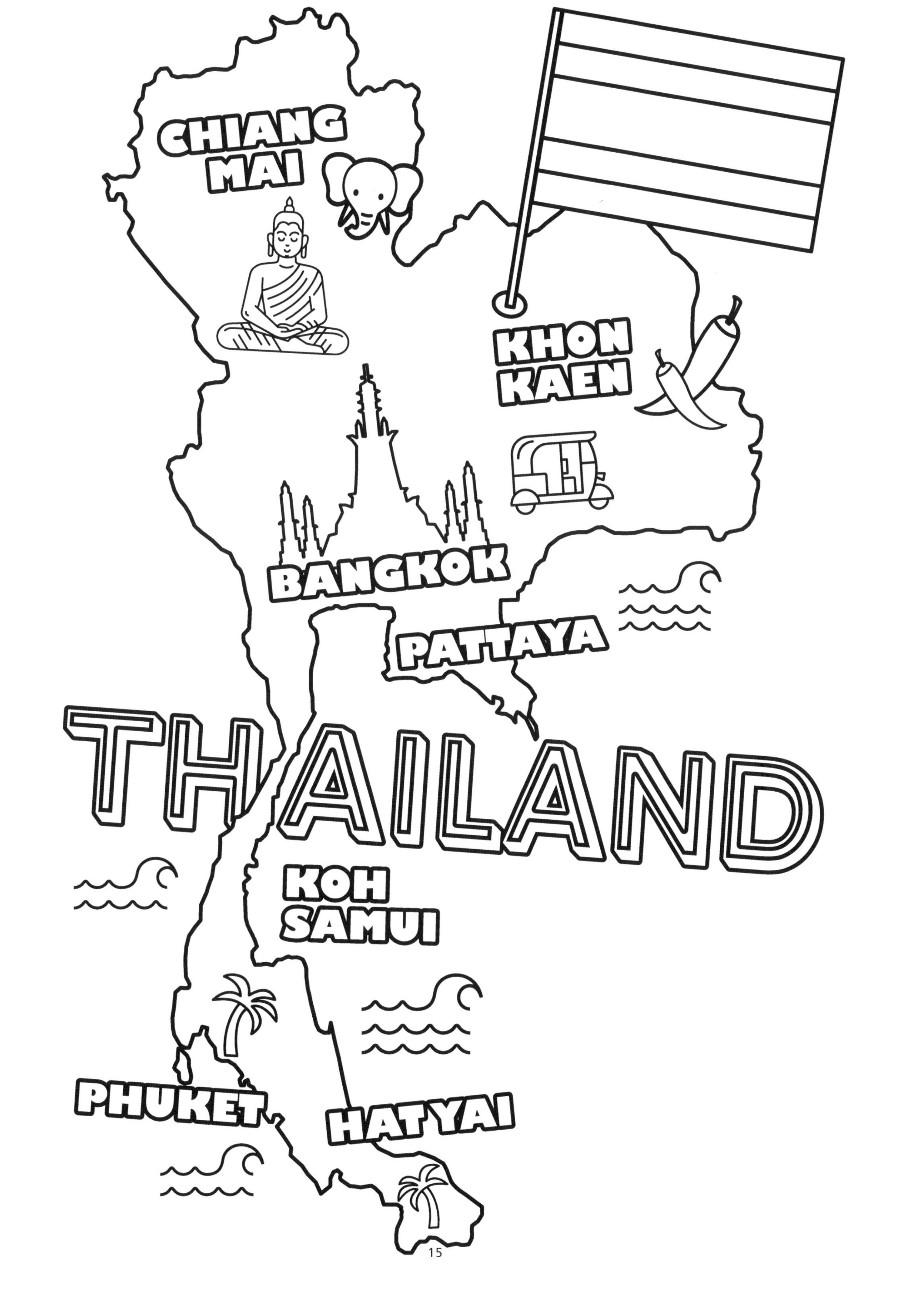
CHIANG MAI
KHON KAEN
BANGKOK
PATTAYA
THAILAND
KOH SAMUI
PHUKET
HATYAI

INVERNESS
GLASGOW
BELFAST
UNITED KINGDOM
BIRMINGHAM
CARDIFF
LONDON

日本
JAPAN
SAPPORO
KYOTO
TOKYO
YOKOHAMA
OSAKA

SAINT PETERSBURG
MOSCOW
NOVOSIBIRSK
RUSSIA

THESSALONIKI
PATRAS
ATHENS
Ελλάδα
CRETE
GREECE

NEW DELHI
KOLKATA
MUMBAI
BANGALORE
CHENNAI
INDIA

ALEXANDRIA
CAIRO
SIWA
OASIS
LUXOR
EGYPT

PRETORIA
JOHANNESBURG
DURBAN
CAPE TOWN
PORT ELIZABETH
SOUTH AFRICA

ORDEM E PROGRESSO
FORTALEZA
BRASILÍA
RIO DE JANEIRO
SAO PAOLO
BRAZIL

BRISBANE
SYDNEY
PERTH
MELBOURNE
AUSTRALIA

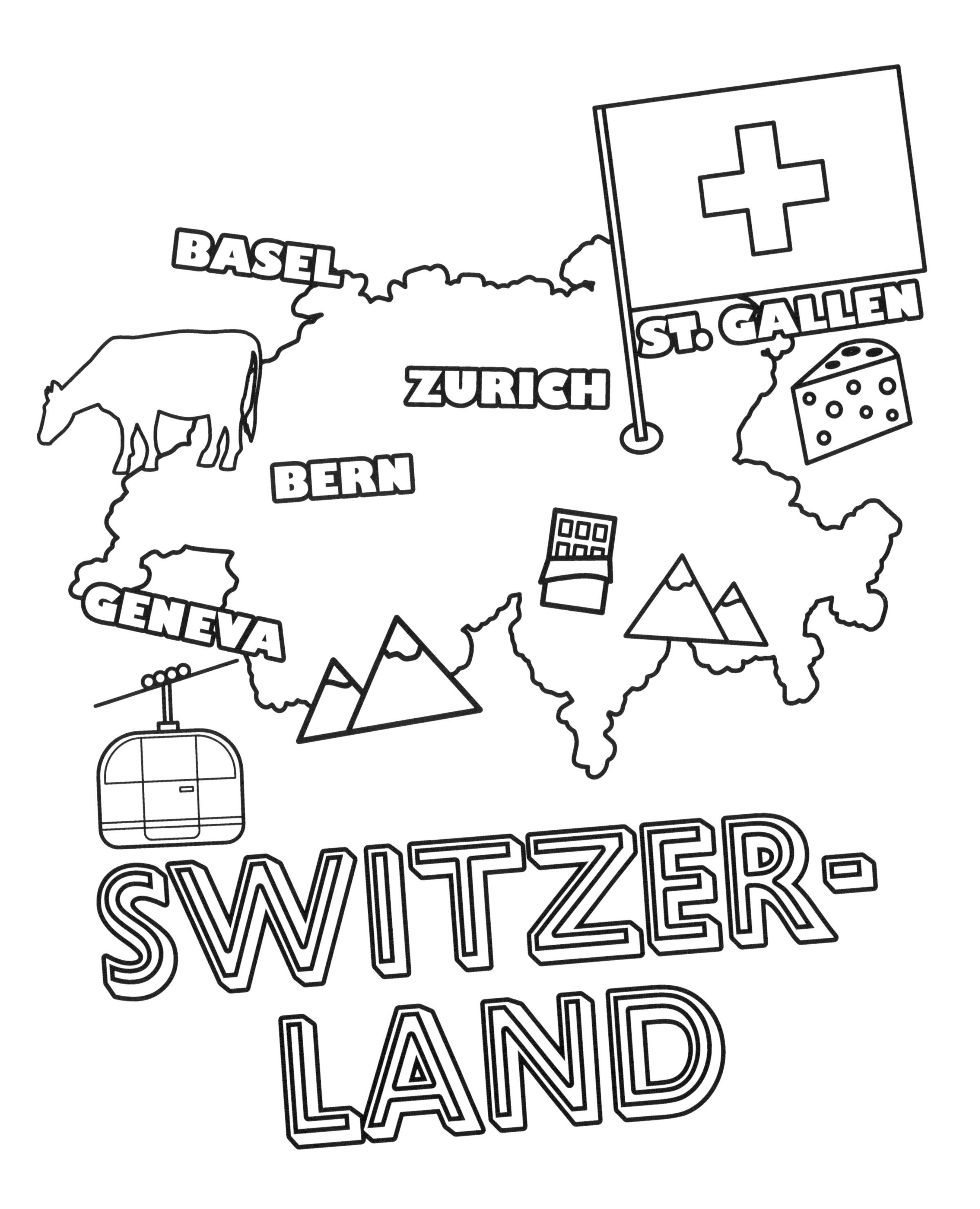
BASEL
ZURICH
ST. GALLEN
BERN
GENEVA
SWITZER-
LAND

CHICLAYO
TRUJILLO
LIMA
CUSCO
PERU
AREQUIPA

ISTANBUL
ANKARA
IZMIR
ANTALYA
TURKEY

WWW.HAPPY-LITTLE-LLAMA.COM

facebook.com/HLLBooks instagram.com/happy.little.llama

Thank you for purchasing this book! If you or your child liked it, we would be very happy about a **review on Amazon**. Honest reviews help us to improve ourselves and our products.

If you are not happy with this book, just send us an email to feedback@happy-little-llama.com and we will try to solve the problem. You are also welcome to contact us if you have any other questions. Be sure to check out our website/our social media channels, too.

Publisher: Marcel Gorgolewski · Matthias Claudius Str. 7a · 21502 Geesthacht, Germany